The True Story of a Mouse who Never Asked for It

Note to Readers

This book is the debut title under Enchanted Lion's 'Unruly'
—a new imprint of picture books for older readers and adults
that are innovative in form and narrative structure.

We have launched Unruly because we believe that the possibilities
for the illustrated book are larger and richer than the categories
that currently exist for it. Unruly celebrates the picture book as
a unique medium of word and picture, relevant and of unsung
value to older readers.

The True Story of a Mouse who Never Asked for It stakes itself
in the liminal zone between youth and adulthood, between picture
book and avant-garde illustrated book.

We hope you enjoy it.

The True Story of a Mouse who Never Asked for It

Ana Cristina Herreros / Violeta Lópiz

Translated from Spanish by Chloe Garcia Roberts
Edited by Sara Elisabeth Paulson

an
Enchanted Lion Book
NEW YORK

To all the mice that once ended up in the claws of a cat. — Ana Cristina Herreros

For Luz. — Violeta Lópiz

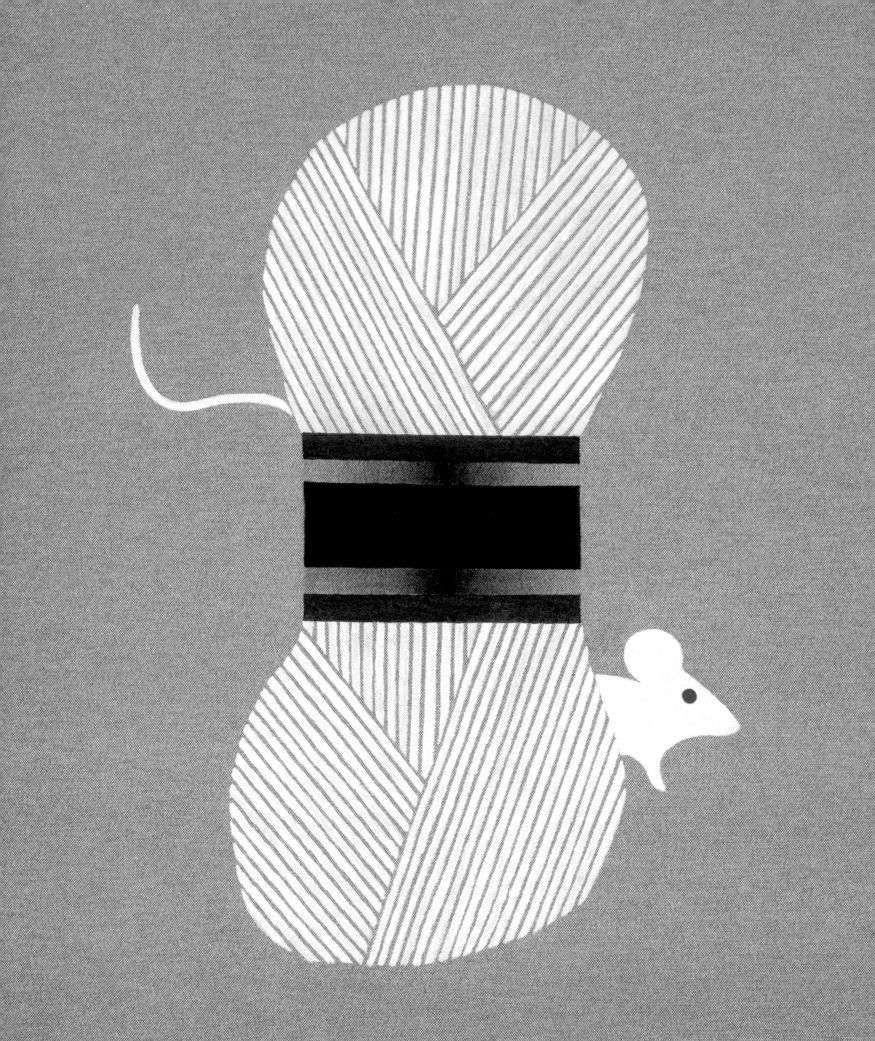

Once upon a time, there was a little mouse who was very neat and very hardworking.

She kept her hair brushed and her doorstep swept clean.

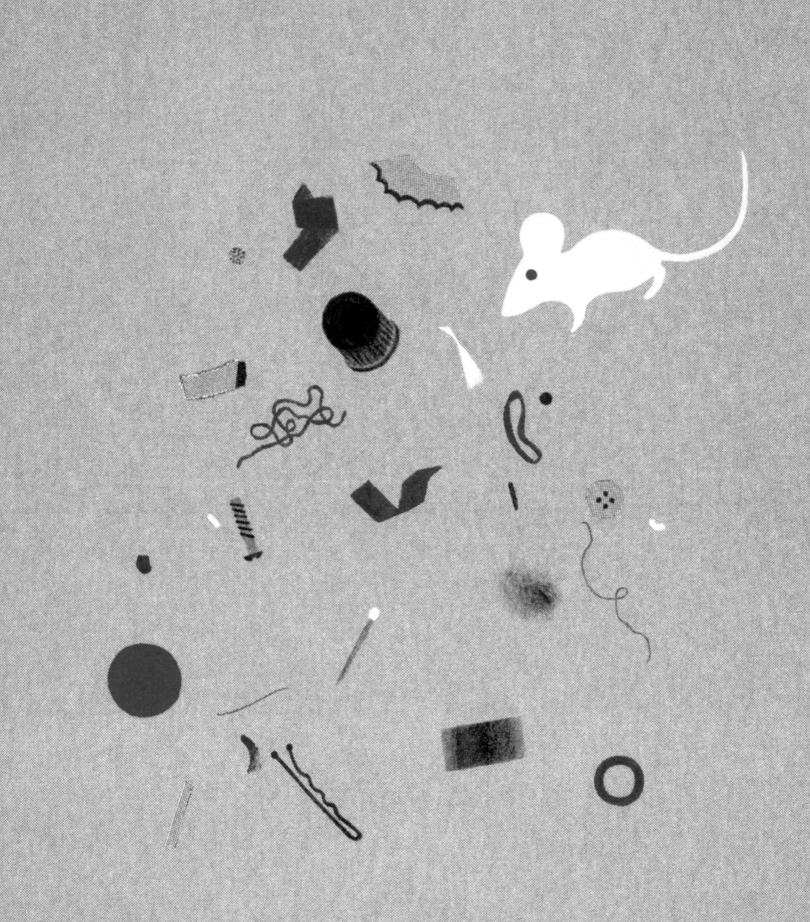

One day, while sweeping up litter on the street,
she found a coin and wondered,
"What shall I buy with this little coin?"

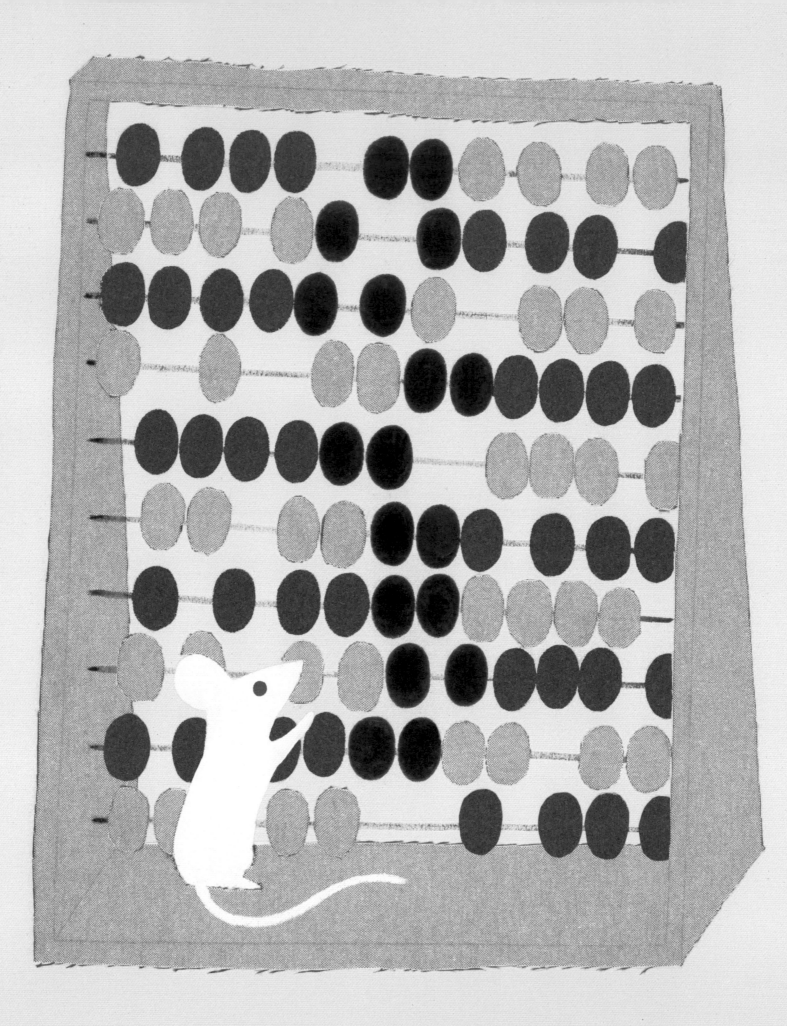

Shall I buy a bag of hazelnuts?
No, I would need to sweep up
all of the little round shells.

Shall I buy a bag of walnuts?
No, I would need to sweep up
all of the big round shells.

Shall I buy a bag of almonds?
No, I would need to sweep up
all of the hard pointy shells.

Enough, I know!
I'll buy a cabbage as round as the globe
and make myself a modest home.

With the cabbage's core, I'll raise the rafters.
From its thick outer leaves, I'll smooth the walls.

And from its fine inner leaves, I'll fashion my bedsheets.

So she said and so she did.

With her house complete, she leaned
over the balcony to look upon the street.

And there she was, when a drove of donkeys came trotting by, and asked her:

"Little mouse, little mouse, you own a house and aren't a wife? Won't you marry one of us?"

"If you can carry a tune, I will marry one of you."

He haw, he haw, he haw, brayed the donkeys.

"My house shudders and me, I shake!
None will I marry, now please go away."

Another day, a flock of ducks came flying by, and asked her:

"Little mouse, little mouse, you own a house and aren't a wife? Won't you marry one of us?"

"If you can carry a tune, I will marry one of you."

Quack, quack, quack, quacked the ducks.

"My house shudders and me, I shake!
None will I marry, now please go away."

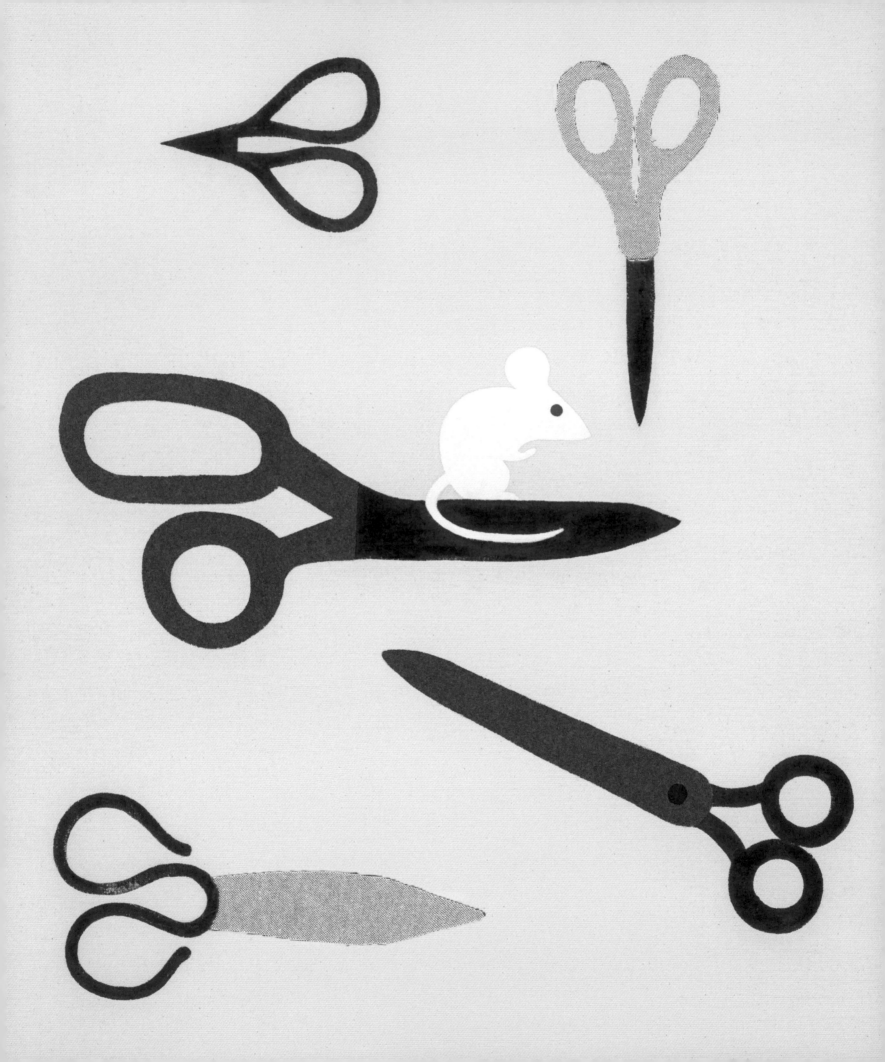

The day after, an abundance of cats came dashing by,
and asked her:

"Little mouse, little mouse, you own a house and aren't a wife?
Won't you marry one of us?"

"If you can carry a tune, I will marry one of you."

Meow, meow, meow, meowed the cats.

"My house shudders and me, I shake!
None will I marry, now please go away."

One fine day, a long line of tiny cats came tiptoeing by,
and at the very end was the frailest one of all.

"Little mouse, little mouse, you own a house and aren't a wife?
Won't you marry one of us?"

"If you can carry a tune, I will marry one of you."

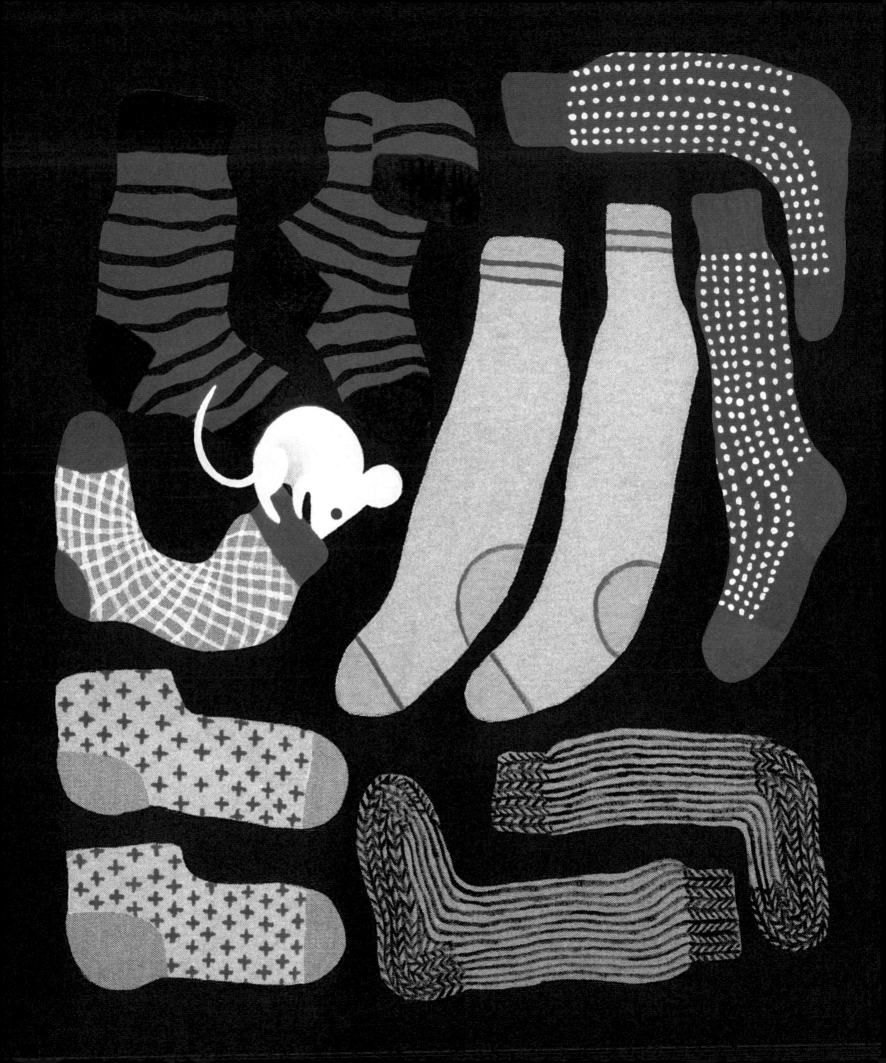

Purr, purr, purr, purred the kittens.

"Come in, please stay! My house sings, and me? I sway!"

"I will marry...that one!" said the mouse, pointing
to the kitten that seemed the most defenseless—
the tiniest one at the back.

And so, the kittens entered her home.

And the mouse married the tiny kitten that was last in line.

They celebrated their wedding that very day,
but the mouse ate cat food, which gave her
a terrible tummyache.

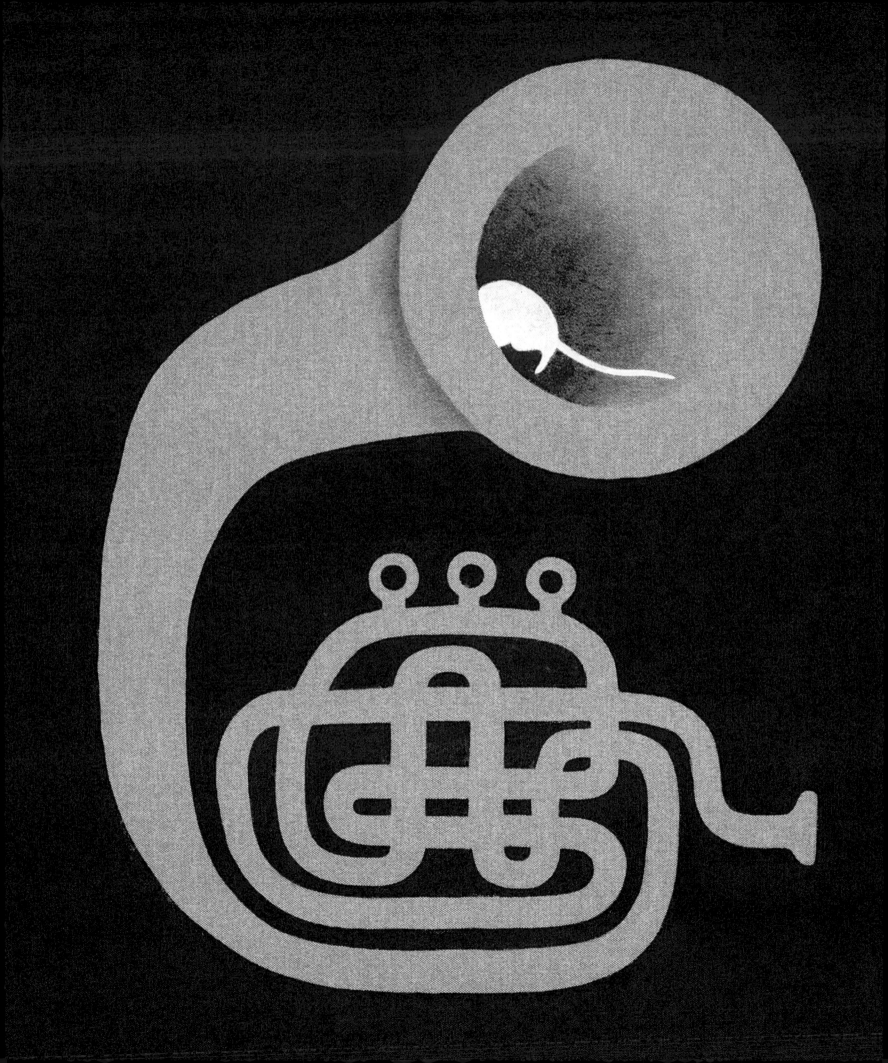

That night, her stomach in knots, she lost it and soiled the sheets.

Being a very clean mouse,
she immediately got up to wash them.

But in the dark, she stumbled, and the sheets tumbled into the washtub. When she leaned over to get a hold of them, she tumbled in, too.

And there she remained, shrieking over her bad luck: "Oh nooo, I'm drowwwning!"

Hearing the mouse's cries, the kitten dragged himself over to the washtub and finding her nearly drowned, asked:

"Little mouse, little mousy, shall I grab you by your foot?"

"No, you'll scratch me."

"Little mouse, little mousy, shall I grab you by your whiskers?"

"No, no, you'll scratch me."

"Little mouse, little mousy, shall I grab you by your ear?"

"No, no, no, you'll scratch me."

Fed up, the tiny kitten grabbed her by the tail and pulled her out without a scratch.

Since the mouse was wet, the kitten dropped her down under the branches of the almond tree and left her there, to dry off and recover from her fright.

But the almonds were ripening, and one pointy shell fell on her face, splitting open her lip.

When the kitten saw that his mouse was hurt,
he began to fret.

"Oh, little mousy, what can I do to fix your lip?
I know! I'll go to the seamstress and ask for thread,
to stitch up the split lip of my little mousy."

And so off went the kitten to look for the seamstress.

"Seamstress, oh seamstress, will you give me some thread
to stitch up the split lip of my little mousy?"

"I'll give you thread for the stitches,
if you give me bristles for a hairbrush."

"And who will give me bristles?"

"The one who lives in a pen and wallows in the mud."

So off went the cat to look for the pig.

"Pig, oh dear piggy, will you give me some bristles?
Bristles to give to the seamstress, who will give me thread
to stitch up the split lip of my little mousy."

"I'll give you bristles for a hairbrush,
if you give me bread for my belly."

"And who will give me bread?"

"The one who works in the bakery
and brings bread to our homes."

So off went the tomcat to look for the baker.

"Baker, oh baker, will you give me some bread?
Bread to give to the pig, who will give me bristles
to give to the seamstress, who will give me thread
to stitch up the split lip of my little mousy."

"I'll give you bread for the pig's belly,
if you give me flour for dough."

"And who will give me flour?"

"The one who grinds wheat to flour
and whose tongue is never sour."

So off went Top Cat to look for the miller.

"Miller, oh miller, will you give me some flour?
Flour to give to the baker, who will give me bread
to give to the pig, who will give me bristles
to give to the seamstress, who will give me thread
to stitch up the split lip of my little mousy."

"I'll give you flour for dough,
if you give me wheat for the mill."

"And who will give me wheat?"

"The one who gives straw and wheat
to those who work hard in the heat."

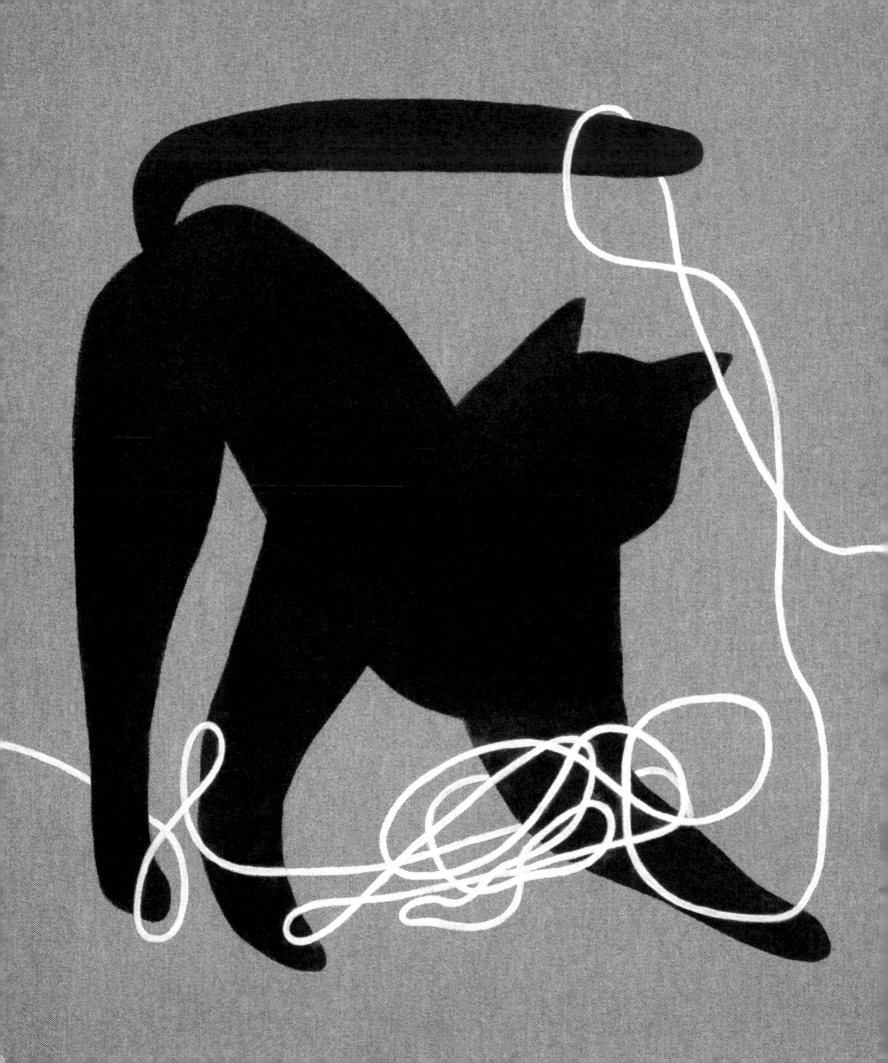

So off went Don Gato to look for the field.

"Field, oh golden field, will you give me some wheat?
Wheat to give to the miller, who will give me flour
to give to the baker, who will give me bread
to give to the pig, who will give me bristles
to give to the seamstress, who will give me thread
to stitch up the split lip of my little mousy."

"I'll give you wheat for the mill,
if you give me water for my thirst."

"And who will give me water?"

"The one forever deep and round
who hides water underground."

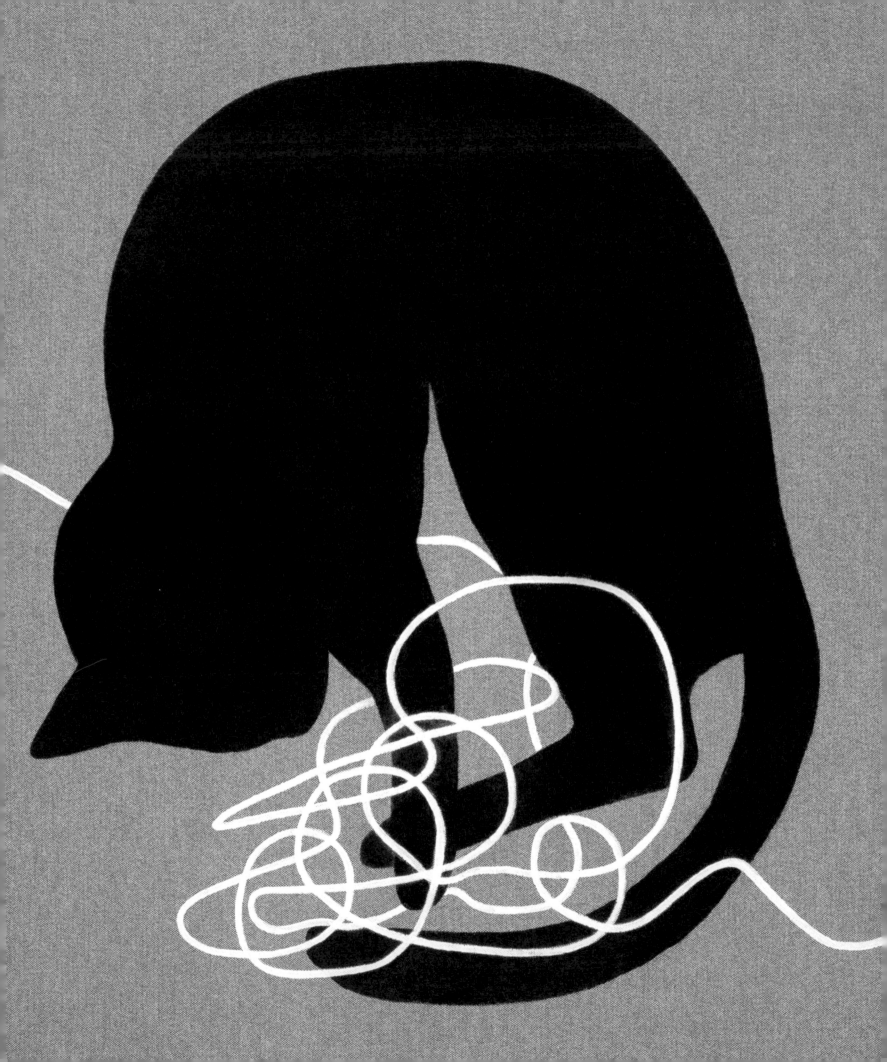

So off stomped Catzilla to look for the well.

"Well, oh wishing well, will you give me some water?
Water to give to the field, who will give me wheat
to give to the miller, who will give me flour
to give to the baker, who will give me bread
to give to the pig, who will give me bristles
to give to the seamstress, who will give me thread
to stitch up the split lip of my little mousy."

"I will give you water for the field's thirst,
if you give me cord for my bucket."

"And who will give me cord?"

"The one who braids tall grassy crops
into tightly twisted rope."

So off tromped Catzón to look for the weaver.

"Weaver, oh weaver, will you braid me some cord?
Cord to give to the well, who will give me water
to give to the field, who will give me wheat
to give to the miller, who will give me flour
to give to the baker, who will give me bread
to give to the pig, who will give me bristles
to give to the seamstress, who will give me thread
to stitch up the split lip of my little mousy."

"No, I won't," said the weaver, "because sometimes
you ask for what you'll never get and you get
what you never asked for."

And so, the kitten, cat, tomcat, Top Cat, Don Gato, Catzilla, Catzón returned to his mouse, his little mousy. Since he didn't have any thread to stitch up her split lip, he gave her a great big lick to clean her wound.

And he liked the taste of the mouse so much...

...he ate her all up.

www.enchantedlion.com

Based on a popular Balearic story

Original English-language edition first published in 2021 by Enchanted Lion Books,
248 Creamer Street, Studio 4, Brooklyn, NY 11231

Printed in Spain by Cofás, Madrid
First Printing

With support from:

G CONSELLERIA
O PRESIDÈNCIA,
I CULTURA I
B IGUALTAT

institut d'estudis
baleàrics